Lydia
the Reading
Fairy

To book-lovers everywhere

Special thanks to
Rachel Elliot

ORCHARD BOOKS
338 Euston Road, London NW1 3BH
Orchard Books Australia
Level 17/207 Kent Street, Sydney, NSW 2000
A Paperback Original

First published in 2014 by Orchard Books

© 2014 Rainbow Magic Limited.
A HIT Entertainment company. Rainbow Magic
is a trademark of Rainbow Magic Limited.
Reg. U.S. Pat. & Tm. Off. And other countries.

HiT entertainment

Illustrations © Orchard Books 2014

A CIP catalogue record for this book is available
from the British Library.

ISBN 978 1 40833 397 6

1 3 5 7 9 10 8 6 4 2

Printed and bound by CPI Group (UK) Ltd, Croydon, CR0 4YY

MIX
Paper from
responsible sources
FSC® C104740

Orchard Books is a division of Hachette Children's Books,
an Hachette UK company

www.hachette.co.uk

Lydia
the Reading
Fairy

by Daisy Meadows

ORCHARD

www.rainbowmagic.co.uk

The Fairyland Palace

Fairyland School

Tippington Town

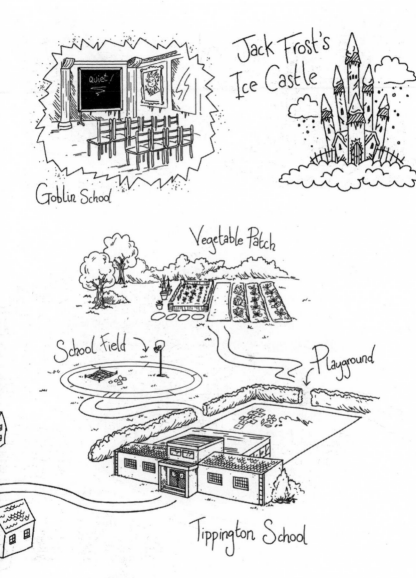

Goblin School

Jack Frost's Ice Castle

Vegetable Patch

School Field

Playground

Tippington School

Jack Frost's Spell

It's time the School Days Fairies see
How wonderful a school should be –
A place where goblins must be bossed,
And learn about the great Jack Frost.

Now every fairy badge of gold
Makes goblins do as they are told.
Let silly fairies whine and wail.
My cleverness will never fail!

Contents

Backwards Books

"I love the smell of libraries, don't you?" said Kirsty Tate.

She took a deep breath and looked around at the bookshelves of the Tippington School library. Her best friend, Rachel Walker, smiled at her.

"I love having you here at school with me," she said. "I wish it was for longer than a week!"

It was only the third day of the new term, and it had already turned into the most fun and exciting term Rachel had ever known. She had lots of friends at Tippington School, but none of them was as special as Kirsty. She had often wished that they could go to the same school. Then Kirsty's school had been flooded, and the builders had said that the repairs were going to take a week. So for five happy days the best friends were at school together at last.

"It's turning into quite a week, though," Kirsty replied with a grin.

Rachel knew that Kirsty was talking about the extraordinary secret they shared. From the time when they had met on Rainspell Island, they had been friends of Fairyland. Even though they had often had magical adventures since then, it was always thrilling to meet brand-new fairy friends. And on the first day of this term, they had been introduced to the School Days Fairies.

"I wonder if we'll see any of the School Days Fairies today," Kirsty whispered.

Before Rachel could reply, her form teacher clapped his hands together to get everyone's attention.

"I want each of you to choose a book to read," said Mr Beaker. "Then write a few sentences about what you think of the book. All the book reports will be included in the display for the school inspector's visit."

"What sort of book should we choose, sir?" asked Adam.

"Try to pick something that you think will transport you to another world," said Mr Beaker. "I love reading, and the best sort of books are the ones where the story comes to life. The people should seem as real to you as your best friend."

The children started to wander around the library, browsing the shelves.

"Be brave in your book choice," Mr Beaker went on. "It might be exciting to pick something that you wouldn't normally read. Surprise yourself!"

There was a loud crash, and Amina and Ellie jumped back from the shelves they had been browsing. Three heavy books had almost landed on top of them.

"Please be careful," said Mr Beaker.

"But sir, they just fell off the shelf," cried Ellie. "We didn't touch them!"

"Sir, this book is stuck shut," said Adam, who was trying to look at a mystery story. "I can't open it."

Rachel had just chosen a book called *The Princess in the Tower*. But when she opened it, none of the sentences made sense. She blinked a few times, wondering if her eyes were playing tricks on her. But there was definitely something very odd about the book.

"Everything is backwards," she whispered to Kirsty. "Listen, this is how the story begins: 'After ever happily lived Rose Princess.' Something

has happened in here.
The books are all
wrong – and I bet
I know why."

Kirsty knew
exactly what her
best friend was
thinking. This
was all happening
because of Jack Frost's
goblins!

When the girls had met Marissa
the Science Fairy on the first day of
term, she had whisked them away to
Fairyland. There, the other School Days
Fairies had explained that Jack Frost had
stolen their magical gold star badges.
Without them, lessons would be boring
and muddled.

"Jack Frost has caused so much trouble for the School Days Fairies," Kirsty said in a low voice. "We've helped Marissa the Science Fairy and Alison the Art Fairy to get their badges back, but we have to find all four of them to make sure everything is perfect for the royal visit."

Queen Titania and King Oberon were planning to pay a visit to the fairy school. The fairies wanted everything to be perfect for their beloved king and queen, but without their magical badges, the royal visit would be a disaster. Not only that, but lessons in the human world would be spoiled too.

Jack Frost had used the magical badges to open a school for goblins, where he was teaching them all about himself. He thought it was the only subject worth learning! But when he had expelled two of his students for being naughty, they had stolen the magical badges from him and taken them to the human world.

And right now, those pesky goblins were in Tippington School!

The girls had soon realised that the two new boys in their class were not really boys at all. Their disguise had fooled Mr Beaker and the other children, but Kirsty and Rachel were very good at spotting goblins.

"We should find the goblins and see what they're doing," Rachel whispered.

Kirsty nodded. Mr Beaker wasn't watching them – he was too busy trying to open Adam's book. The girls made their way towards the back of the library, where the lights were dim and the least-borrowed books were kept. Not many pupils looked in this section, but now the girls could hear loud, screechy voices. They looked at each other.

"Goblins," they said together.

They peered around a tall bookshelf and saw the two goblins sitting cross-legged on the floor.

Each of them
was holding
a book and
reading
aloud.
They
didn't
seem to care
that the other one
wasn't listening.

"Once upon a time
there was a grumpy troll
who liked to eat princes and princesses,"
read the first goblin in a loud voice.
"But there weren't enough princes and
princesses to fill him up. So he decided
to go on holiday with his best friend, a
handsome goblin."

"Milly, Tilly and Gilly were sisters,"

read the second goblin in an equally loud voice. "They were human beings, and so of course they were very stupid and annoying and ugly. One day a happy little goblin was stealing some apples when the sisters decided to poke their silly noses in."

"They just love the sound of their own voices, don't they!" said Rachel.

"Yes," said Kirsty with a frown, "and it sounds as if those stories have been changed – they don't sound right at all."

Just then they heard footsteps coming up from behind them and whirled around. Mr Beaker was coming their way. When he saw the girls and heard the voices, he stopped. Rachel and Kirsty thought that he might tell the goblins off, but he just smiled.

"I'm glad to hear someone in the class is enjoying their books," he said. "I don't know what's gone wrong, but reading doesn't seem to be very much fun today."

"Do you want us to ask them to talk more quietly, sir?" Kirsty asked.

Mr Beaker shook his head.

"It's nice to hear that they're so enthusiastic," he said. "I don't mind a bit of noise now and then."

As he walked away, the girls exchanged a surprised glance.

"I suppose the main thing is that they're not causing any trouble," said Rachel. "For now!"

"Look at that bookshelf over there," said Kirsty.

She pointed to a bookshelf in the corner. One of the shelves seemed to be gleaming with a faint light, and the girls hurried towards it.

"The light must be coming from one of the books on this shelf," said Rachel.

"It looks just like a fairy glow."

They searched through the books that were on the shelf until they found one that was shimmering with a golden light.

"This must be the one," said Rachel, taking it down from the shelf. She opened it, and out fluttered Lydia the Reading Fairy! Her black hair was tied in a thick side plait, and she was wearing flowery shorts with a pink jumper and a cute little hat.

"Hello, Rachel! Hello, Kirsty!" said Lydia. "Queen Titania told me that you were in the library, and I thought it was the perfect moment to ask for your help."

"So you still haven't found your magical gold star badge?" Kirsty asked.

Lydia shook her head.

"I'm sure it must be around here somewhere," she said. "Please will you help me to find it? Children all over the world have stopped enjoying reading, and it's all because of those naughty goblins."

"Of course we'll help," said Rachel. "Lydia, the goblins are here in the library right now, and no one is watching us. Shall we go and ask them to give your badge back?"

Lydia nodded at once.

"I'm a bit nervous of Jack Frost, but I'm not scared of goblins," she said. "Let's go and talk to them right now."

She hid in Rachel's pocket and then the girls walked back to the tall bookshelf where the goblins were reading.

But before they got there, Kirsty clutched at Rachel's arm.

"Look!" she whispered. "Between those books!"

In a gap between some books on a shelf, the girls could see an ice-blue robe and a mortarboard hat. Holding their breath, they tiptoed up to the shelf and peeped through the gap. Then they stared at each other in shock.

Jack Frost was in their school!

A Rhyming Spell and a Reading

Jack Frost was creeping along beside the shelves towards the goblins. They hadn't noticed him because they were so interested in their books. They were still reading aloud.

"The grumpy troll and the handsome goblin snowboarded down the snowy mountain," the first goblin was reading at the top of his voice. "Everyone gasped, because they had never seen such amazing skill and speed. They were better than Olympic athletes and faster than fairies."

"The goblin found a really clever hiding place for the apples," bellowed the second goblin. "But Milly, Tilly and Gilly cheated and spied on him, and they took the apples back to the orchard. So the goblin locked them in an ice castle for a hundred years, and that served them right."

"BOO!" shouted Jack Frost, leaping out in front of them.

The goblins jumped up in fright, dropping the books on the floor. Jack Frost walked slowly towards them, and they backed away until they hit a bookshelf.

"I'm here for my magical badge," he said. "You scrawny little halfwits are going to give it to me — right now!"

He pulled a blue book out from under his robe. Rachel and Kirsty could see the title clearly, because it was written in shining silver letters: *Fantastic Jack Frost, The Story of My Life.*

"This is the best book in the world," he said. "I want every single goblin in my school to hear the story, but none of them is paying attention and it's all your fault!"

He was shaking with rage, and the goblins' knees started to knock together.

"W-w-what can we d-d-do, Your Iciness?" asked the first goblin.

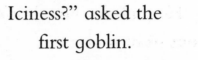

The second goblin opened his mouth to speak but couldn't get any words out, so gave a little curtsy instead.

"Give me the badge, numbskull!" Jack Frost roared.

Trembling, the first goblin put his hand into his pocket and pulled out a shining golden badge.

"That's it!" said Lydia. "My badge!"

But before the girls could do anything, Jack Frost had snatched the badge and disappeared in a crack of blue lightning!

"Quick, use your magic!" Rachel begged Lydia. "We have to catch up with Jack Frost!"

Lydia fluttered out of Rachel's pocket and hovered in front of them, holding up her wand and speaking the words of a spell.

"Follow Jack Frost without any delay

*To find the gold badge he has stolen
away.*

*Whether in sunshine or whether in
snow,*

Take us wherever he chooses to go."

With a whooshing sound, a ribbon
of sparkling fairy dust wound
around the girls,
wrapping them
in magic.
They closed
their eyes
and their
shoulder
blades
tingled as
gossamer
wings appeared.

They heard the tinkle of far-off silver bells, and then felt a blast of ice-cold air. When they opened their eyes, they were standing inside a very different sort of library.

Icicles were hanging from the shelves, and there were patches of ice on the threadbare carpet. But the strangest thing was that every book in the library was exactly the same. Row after row, the girls gazed at thousands of copies of a large, blue book with the title written in silver letters. *Fantastic Jack Frost, The Story of My Life.* They were inside the library of Jack Frost's Ice Castle!

The girls and Lydia were standing between two rows of bookshelves. Before they could say a word, they saw Jack Frost striding across the front of the library. A crowd of goblin pupils was sitting on the carpet in front of him.

"Hide!" said Kirsty with a gasp.

They fluttered over to hide behind a bookshelf at the back of the library, close to the door.

"I thought Jack Frost said that the goblins weren't paying attention," Rachel whispered. "They all look very well behaved to me."

"There's a good reason for that," said Lydia, looking serious. "Look at what he's wearing on his robe."

The girls peered through the shelves and saw Lydia's magical badge glittering on Jack Frost's robe.

"That's why the goblins are being so good," said Kirsty.

They watched as Jack opened a copy of his book and started to read.

"Chapter one," he began. "The fairies have always caused trouble for me, and their stupid sense of right and wrong is always getting in my way. One day, I decided that enough was enough. My

brilliant brain instantly thought of
a fantastic plan to stop them, once and
for all!"

Jack Frost was a terribly boring reader.
He didn't change the tone of his voice
at all. He just droned on and on, and
soon the girls were yawning, but the
goblins kept listening as if the story
was the most wonderful thing that they
had ever heard.

"We have to do something to stop
him before we all fall asleep," said
Lydia. "We must get the badge back
— but *how*?"

Punished!

Rachel looked around and spotted a bell hanging on a hook by the library door. She tapped Kirsty on the shoulder and pointed at the bell.

"Jack Frost must ring that bell as the signal for break time," she said. "We'd have a much better chance of getting the badge back from him if the goblins were playing outside. But first, Kirsty and I need to look like goblins."

Lydia held up her wand.

"Let my spell hide both these faces,
Cast away all human graces.
Disguise my friends as goblins green,
And let no fairy wings be seen."

The girls felt a creeping,
tickling feeling as
their clothes were
replaced with
green goblin
uniforms. Their
noses and ears
grew long and
pointy, and their
hair shrank away
until they were
bald.

"Rachel, you look terrible!" said Kirsty with a giggle.

"You too!" said Rachel, giving her a hug. "I'm glad it's only for a short while."

They made their way over to the library door, hoping that Jack Frost wouldn't see them. Luckily he was still busy reading all about himself. They could hear his voice booming out.

"That was when I generously decided to give some goblins the chance to be my servants," he declared. "I visited the goblin village and chose the least stupid and the least ugly of them all. They all kissed my hands in thanks."

"This is definitely not a good story," said Rachel.

She reached up and rang the bell as

loudly as she could. At the front of the library, Jack Frost jumped in surprise and stopped reading. The goblins scrambled to their feet and there was a stampede for the door.

"Let me out!" Kirsty heard one of them mutter.

"What a load of rubbish," whispered another.

"I couldn't stop listening," said a third. "Something was forcing me to be good. It was awful."

They pushed and shoved each other aside, trying to reach the door first. Rachel and Kirsty had to run to get out of their way, but in the confusion they ran in the wrong direction – straight into the arms of Jack Frost!

Jack Frost pinched one of Kirsty's goblin ears between his thumb and his forefinger. He did the same to Rachel, frowning at them.

47

"I saw what you two did!" he snapped. "You rang the playtime bell too early! You interrupted the amazing story of my life! You're going to be punished for that!"

"We're very sorry," said Kirsty, trying to whimper like a real goblin. "Please don't punish us!"

But Jack Frost was furious, and he wouldn't let go of their ears.

"You will miss out on playtime," he said. "You will have to sit in my office and work. Come on!"

Rachel and Kirsty exchanged a hopeful glance. Perhaps this was their chance to get Lydia's badge back!

Pulling Rachel and Kirsty along by the ears, Jack Frost marched them out of the library and along a dim, damp corridor to his office. There was a brass sign on the door.

Jack Frost
Headmaster and Genius

By twisting her head around, Rachel could see that Lydia was hovering behind them in the shadows. Jack Frost kicked the door open and shoved the girls inside. Then he marched around to the chair behind his desk and sat down. Lydia

just had time to slip
inside the room
before the door
banged shut.
Kirsty saw her
hide behind a
large plant pot.
It contained a very
droopy looking cactus.

"You two are going to learn that when
I'm talking, you should be listening,"
said Jack Frost, drumming his long
fingers on his desk. "You should have
been paying attention in class. So I want
you to write a whole page each about
why *Fantastic Jack Frost, The Story of
My Life* is the best book ever."

"Oh, thank you, sir!" exclaimed
Kirsty, much to Rachel's surprise.

"That's a wonderful assignment. I could talk for days about your book. It is so exciting! You must be so clever to have written it."

A smile flickered around Jack Frost's grumpy mouth, and Rachel suddenly guessed Kirsty's idea. If they could distract Jack Frost, perhaps Lydia would be able to unpin the badge from his robe.

Hop, Skip and Jump

"You must have had a really interesting life," said Rachel. "I can't wait to finish reading your amazing book."

"I'm just naturally gifted," said Jack Frost, stroking his spiky beard.

"Will you sign some copies of your book for us?" asked Kirsty, clasping her hands together.

"Very well, very well," said Jack Frost. He sounded almost kind. There was a big pile of his books on the table, and he opened one and began to sign his name with a leaky fountain pen. Lydia swooped down, ducked under his arm and started to undo the pin. But just as he finished signing the second book, the fountain pen squirted a blob of ink onto Jack Frost's robe. He glanced down – and saw Lydia trying to take the badge!

"A FAIRY IN MY OFFICE?"
bellowed Jack Frost. "How dare you!
I'll put you in detention! I'll give you a
year's worth of homework! I'll make you
sit exams every day! COME HERE!"

He tried to trap Lydia between his
hands, but she zoomed away from him
and out through the open window. Jack
Frost hurled himself after her, his long
robe flapping behind him as he ran.

"They're heading for the playground," cried Rachel. "Come on – we have to stop him from catching Lydia!"

She and Kirsty clambered out of the window too, and followed Jack Frost towards the icy playground. He was still yelling at Lydia, but now he was panting too, because he was so unfit. Rachel and Kirsty reached the playground and only just avoided skidding into some goblins playing hopscotch.

"Watch it!" the goblins yelled rudely.

The girls really wanted to say sorry, but they knew that a real goblin would never be that polite! They stuck out their tongues and the other goblins did the same.

"YOWCH!" squealed a tall, lanky goblin.

A plump, warty goblin had landed
on his foot. But as he hopped around,
clutching his toes, he tripped over
a goblin with a skipping rope. They
both fell flat on their faces, tangled in
the rope.

"You idiot!" they screeched at each
other.

Rachel clutched Kirsty's arm.

"Those clumsy goblins have given me an idea," she said. "Maybe our big goblin feet can trip Jack Frost up."

"Let's try it!" Kirsty said in an eager voice.

They raced after Jack Frost, who was sprinting around the playground, snatching at the fairy fluttering in front of him. Lydia zigzagged left and right, and it was hard to keep up with them, but at last the girls were close enough to touch Jack Frost's trailing robe.

"Ready...steady...JUMP!" shouted Rachel.

They sprang through the air and landed on the hem of the long, blue robe with their big feet. The robe was yanked off and Jack Frost staggered sideways,

lost his footing and
tumbled into
a snowy
sandpit.

Lydia
looped
the loop
in mid-
air and
swooped
down to the
robe. She unpinned
the gold star badge before Jack Frost
could clamber to his feet, and then
zoomed out of his reach.

"Give it back!" screamed Jack Frost,
stamping his feet and waving his fists in
the air. "You tricksy little fairy! Give me
my badge!"

"It's *my* badge," said Lydia in her gentle voice. "And now I've got it back, thanks to my friends, children all over the world will be able to enjoy reading again."

As she spoke, Rachel and Kirsty's disguises melted away and they fluttered upwards to join Lydia. Jack Frost turned a very strange purple colour as he realised he had been tricked. He snatched up his robe, stomped over to the outside bell and rang it crossly.

"Everyone inside – NOW!" he
bellowed. "If I can't have any fun, then
neither can you!

The goblins grumbled and hung
back. None of them wanted to listen
to another reading from Jack Frost's
book. But their headmaster was looking
especially fierce, so one by one they all
shuffled back into school. Lydia, Kirsty
and Rachel hovered in the air and
watched them.

"Are we
going to
take the
badge back
to the fairy
school now?"
Kirsty asked, after the
last goblin had gone inside.

"Well..." said Lydia. "Perhaps it's silly, but I actually feel a bit sorry for Jack Frost. After all, he went to all the trouble of writing a book, and now no one wants to read it."

The girls understood how the kind little fairy was feeling.

"Maybe there's something we can do to help," said Rachel. "Shall we go back to the library and find out?"

The others nodded at once, and together they flew back into the goblin school. There was a terrible noise coming from the library. Goblins were squawking, shrieking and thundering around like a herd of elephants. Jack Frost was sitting at a desk with his head in his hands. Lydia looked around and folded her arms.

"The trouble with these pupils is that they are bored," she said. "What's the use of a library where every book is the same? I've got an idea!"

The Goblin School Library

Lydia flew up to the centre of the ceiling and waved her wand in a wide circle. As a shower of fairy dust rained down onto the library shelves, she recited a spell.

"Transform this room into a place
Of wondrous books and reading space.
Books you read 'til lights go out.
Books you tell your friends about.

Princesses young and witches old,
Adventures wild and heroes bold.
Books that make you laugh out loud,
Real-life tales to make you proud.
Stories that can break your heart.
Stories that are works of art.
Poems, plays and novels too.
Fill these dreary shelves anew!"

As she spoke, the endless copies of *Fantastic Jack Frost, The Story of My Life* began to change. One by one, a colourful selection of books appeared, of all shapes and sizes. As the goblins started to notice and talk about it, Jack Frost looked up. He groaned when he saw all the copies of his book disappearing.

Rachel and Kirsty flew over to land on the desk in front of Jack Frost.

He scowled at them.

"What do you want?" he demanded.

"We'd like to have the copies of your book that you signed for us earlier," said Rachel, trying to sound brave.

Jack Frost's mouth fell open. He stared at them for a moment. Then he stood up and hurried off to fetch the books. While he was gone, the goblins grew quieter and quieter. One by one, they were discovering exciting books and settling down to read them. By the time Jack Frost returned, the goblins were completely quiet.

"There," said Jack Frost, shoving the copies of his book at Rachel and Kirsty.

But he didn't sound quite as cross as usual!

Just then, a very small goblin tapped him on the shoulder.

"I thought you might like this book, sir," said the goblin in a shaky voice.

He held out a copy of *The Snow Queen.* Jack Frost grabbed it and read the back cover.

"Aha!" he exclaimed. "She sounds like my kind of royal!"

He sat down and started reading. With a smile, Lydia landed on the desk beside Rachel and Kirsty.

"You've been wonderful," she said. "Thank you from the bottom of my heart. But now it's time for us all to go home."

The girls kissed her goodbye. Then, in a flurry of magical sparkles, they were lifted into the air. Brushing

fairy dust from their eyes, they blinked…
and found themselves sitting in their
classroom at Tippington School.

Everyone was busy writing about
the books they had chosen. Kirsty
and Rachel looked down and smiled.
There was a copy of *Fantastic Jack
Frost, The Story of My Life* in front of
each of them.

"I think it's time to write a book
report!" Rachel whispered.

In a short while, Mr Beaker cleared his throat.

"All right, everyone," he said. "I'd like to hear what you thought about your books. Let's start with Rachel Walker."

Rachel and Kirsty stood up together.

"We chose the same book," Rachel explained. "It's all about someone called Fantastic Jack Frost. I liked this book because the main character  tries to be scary, but sometimes he's very funny without even knowing it."

"I like the way all the characters come to life in the book," Kirsty added. "You could almost believe that Fairyland and the king and queen really do exist."

Rachel shared a secret smile with her best friend.

"Well, it sounds like a really interesting book," said Mr Beaker. "I've never heard of it before, but you've made me want to read it. I think that the school inspector will be very impressed with your reports when he visits."

Kirsty and Rachel sat down again as Adam started to read his book report.

"In all the excitement I forgot about the inspector coming," Rachel whispered. "I hope we can find the last magical gold star badge before he arrives, or the whole visit will go wrong."

Kirsty nodded, and gave a little smile. "Don't you know?" she said. "All fairy stories end happily ever after!"

Now it's time for Kirsty and Rachel to help...

Kathryn the PE Fairy

Read on for a sneak peek...

"I can't believe that tomorrow is our last day at school together," said Kirsty Tate. "It's been a wonderful week – I wish it didn't have to end."

Rachel Walker squeezed her hand as they sat next to each other in the school hall. The best friends had loved every moment of the past week. Kirsty's school had been flooded, so she had joined Rachel in Tippington.

"It's good that your school will be open again next week, but I am going to miss you so much!" said Rachel.

They were sitting with the rest of Mr

Beaker's class for afternoon assembly.
Miss Patel, the headteacher, clapped her
hands together and everyone fell silent.

"Good afternoon, everyone," she said.
"I hope that you have all had a good
morning and are looking forward to this
afternoon's lessons."

Read **Kathryn the PE Fairy** to find out
what adventures are in store for Kirsty and Rachel!

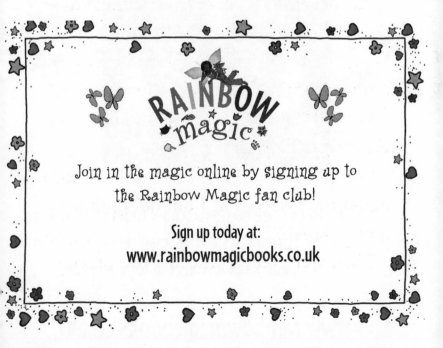

Join in the magic online by signing up to
the Rainbow Magic fan club!

Sign up today at:
www.rainbowmagicbooks.co.uk

Meet the
School Days Fairies

Kirsty and Rachel are going to school together! Can they get back the School Days Fairies' magical objects from Jack Frost, and keep lessons fun for everyone?

www.rainbowmagicbooks.co.uk

Competition!

The School Days Fairies have created a special
competition just for you!

Collect all four books in the School Days Fairies series
and answer the special questions in the back of each one.

Once you have all the answers, take the first letter from
each one and arrange them to spell a secret word!
When you have the answer, go online and enter!

**What type of magical animal
does Leona look after?**

_ _ _ _ _ _ _

We will put all the correct entries into a draw and select
a winner to receive a special Rainbow Magic Goody Bag
featuring lots of treats for you and your fairy friends.
You'll also feature in a new Rainbow Magic story!

Enter online now at www.rainbowmagicbooks.co.uk

No purchase required. Only one entry per child. Two prize draws will take place on
1st April 2015 and 2nd July 2015. Alternatively readers can send the answer on a postcard to:
Rainbow Magic, School Days Fairies Competition,
Orchard Books, 338 Euston Road, London, NW1 3BH. Australian readers can write to:
Rainbow Magic, School Days Fairies Competition, Hachette Children's Books,
level 17/207 Kent St, Sydney, NSW 2000. E-mail: childrens.books@hachette.com.au.
New Zealand readers should write to:
Rainbow Magic, School Days Fairies Competition,
PO Box 3255, Shortland St, Auckland 1140

Have you read them all?

The Rainbow Fairies
1. Ruby the Red Fairy ☐
2. Amber the Orange Fairy ☐
3. Saffron the Yellow Fairy ☐
4. Fern the Green Fairy ☐
5. Sky the Blue Fairy ☐
6. Izzy the Indigo Fairy ☐
7. Heather the Violet Fairy ☐

The Weather Fairies
8. Crystal the Snow Fairy ☐
9. Abigail the Breeze Fairy ☐
10. Pearl the Cloud Fairy ☐
11. Goldie the Sunshine Fairy ☐
12. Evie the Mist Fairy ☐
13. Storm the Lightning Fairy ☐
14. Hayley the Rain Fairy ☐

The Party Fairies
15. Cherry the Cake Fairy ☐
16. Melodie the Music Fairy ☐
17. Grace the Glitter Fairy ☐
18. Honey the Sweet Fairy ☐
19. Polly the Party Fun Fairy ☐
20. Phoebe the Fashion Fairy ☐
21. Jasmine the Present Fairy ☐

The Jewel Fairies
22. India the Moonstone Fairy ☐
23. Scarlett the Garnet Fairy ☐
24. Emily the Emerald Fairy ☐
25. Chloe the Topaz Fairy ☐
26. Amy the Amethyst Fairy ☐
27. Sophie the Sapphire Fairy ☐
28. Lucy the Diamond Fairy ☐

The Pet Keeper Fairies
29. Katie the Kitten Fairy ☐
30. Bella the Bunny Fairy ☐
31. Georgia the Guinea Pig Fairy ☐
32. Lauren the Puppy Fairy ☐
33. Harriet the Hamster Fairy ☐
34. Molly the Goldfish Fairy ☐
35. Penny the Pony Fairy ☐

The Fun Day Fairies
36. Megan the Monday Fairy
37. Tallulah the Tuesday Fairy
38. Willow the Wednesday Fairy
39. Thea the Thursday Fairy
40. Freya the Friday Fairy
41. Sienna the Saturday Fairy
42. Sarah the Sunday Fairy

The Petal Fairies
43. Tia the Tulip Fairy
44. Pippa the Poppy Fairy
45. Louise the Lily Fairy
46. Charlotte the Sunflower Fairy
47. Olivia the Orchid Fairy
48. Danielle the Daisy Fairy
49. Ella the Rose Fairy

The Dance Fairies
50. Bethany the Ballet Fairy
51. Jade the Disco Fairy
52. Rebecca the Rock'n'Roll Fairy
53. Tasha the Tap Dance Fairy
54. Jessica the Jazz Fairy
55. Saskia the Salsa Fairy
56. Imogen the Ice Dance Fairy

The Sporty Fairies
57. Helena the Horseriding Fairy
58. Francesca the Football Fairy
59. Zoe the Skating Fairy
60. Naomi the Netball Fairy
61. Samantha the Swimming Fairy
62. Alice the Tennis Fairy
63. Gemma the Gymnastics Fairy

The Music Fairies
64. Poppy the Piano Fairy
65. Ellie the Guitar Fairy
66. Fiona the Flute Fairy
67. Danni the Drum Fairy
68. Maya the Harp Fairy
69. Victoria the Violin Fairy
70. Sadie the Saxophone Fairy

The Magical Animal Fairies

71. Ashley the Dragon Fairy ☐
72. Lara the Black Cat Fairy ☐
73. Erin the Firebird Fairy ☐
74. Rihanna the Seahorse Fairy ☐
75. Sophia the Snow Swan Fairy ☐
76. Leona the Unicorn Fairy ☐
77. Caitlin the Ice Bear Fairy ☐

The Green Fairies

78. Nicole the Beach Fairy ☐
79. Isabella the Air Fairy ☐
80. Edie the Garden Fairy ☐
81. Coral the Reef Fairy ☐
82. Lily the Rainforest Fairy ☐
83. Carrie the Snow Cap Fairy ☐
84. Milly the River Fairy ☐

The Ocean Fairies

85. Ally the Dolphin Fairy ☐
86. Amelie the Seal Fairy ☐
87. Pia the Penguin Fairy ☐
88. Tess the Sea Turtle Fairy ☐
89. Stephanie the Starfish Fairy ☐
90. Whitney the Whale Fairy ☐
91. Courtney the Clownfish Fairy ☐

The Twilight Fairies

92. Ava the Sunset Fairy ☐
93. Lexi the Firefly Fairy ☐
94. Zara the Starlight Fairy ☐
95. Morgan the Midnight Fairy ☐
96. Yasmin the Night Owl Fairy ☐
97. Maisie the Moonbeam Fairy ☐
98. Sabrina the Sweet Dreams Fairy ☐

The Showtime Fairies

99. Madison the Magic Show Fairy ☐
100. Leah the Theatre Fairy ☐
101. Alesha the Acrobat Fairy ☐
102. Darcey the Dance Diva Fairy ☐
103. Taylor the Talent Show Fairy ☐
104. Amelia the Singing Fairy ☐
105. Isla the Ice Star Fairy ☐

The Princess Fairies

106. Honor the Happy Days Fairy ☐
107. Demi the Dressing-Up Fairy ☐
108. Anya the Cuddly Creatures Fairy ☐
109. Elisa the Adventure Fairy ☐
110. Lizzie the Sweet Treats Fairy ☐
111. Maddie the Playtime Fairy ☐
112. Eva the Enchanted Ball Fairy ☐

The Pop Star Fairies

113. Jessie the Lyrics Fairy ☐
114. Adele the Singing Coach Fairy ☐
115. Vanessa the Dance Steps Fairy ☐
116. Miley the Stylist Fairy ☐
117. Frankie the Make-Up Fairy ☐
118. Rochelle the Star Spotter Fairy ☐
119. Una the Concert Fairy ☐

The Fashion Fairies

120. Miranda the Beauty Fairy ☐
121. Claudia the Accessories Fairy ☐
122. Tyra the Dress Designer Fairy ☐
123. Alexa the Fashion Reporter Fairy ☐
124. Matilda the Hair Stylist Fairy ☐
125. Brooke the Photographer Fairy ☐
126. Lola the Fashion Fairy ☐

The Sweet Fairies

127. Lottie the Lollipop Fairy ☐
128. Esme the Ice Cream Fairy ☐
129. Coco the Cupcake Fairy ☐
130. Clara the Chocolate Fairy ☐
131. Madeleine the Cookie Fairy ☐
132. Layla the Candyfloss Fairy ☐
133. Nina the Birthday Cake Fairy ☐

The Baby Animal Rescue Fairies

134. Mae the Panda Fairy ☐
135. Kitty the Tiger Fairy ☐
136. Mara the Meerkat Fairy ☐
137. Savannah the Zebra Fairy ☐
138. Kimberley the Koala Fairy ☐
139. Rosie the Honey Bear Fairy ☐
140. Anna the Arctic Fox Fairy ☐

The Magical Crafts Fairies

141. Kayla the Pottery Fairy ☐
142. Annabelle the Drawing Fairy ☐
143. Zadie the Sewing Fairy ☐
144. Josie the Jewellery-Making Fairy ☐
145. Violet the Painting Fairy ☐
146. Libby the Story-Writing Fairy ☐
147. Roxie the Baking Fairy ☐

The School Days Fairies

141. Marissa the Science Fairy ☐
142. Alison the Art Fairy ☐
143. Lydia the Reading Fairy ☐
144. Kathryn the PE Fairy ☐

Giselle the Christmas Ballet Fairy

Meet Giselle the Christmas Ballet Fairy! Can Rachel and Kirsty help get her magical items back from Jack Frost in time for the Fairyland Christmas Eve performance?

www.rainbowmagicbooks.co.uk